this book belongs to:

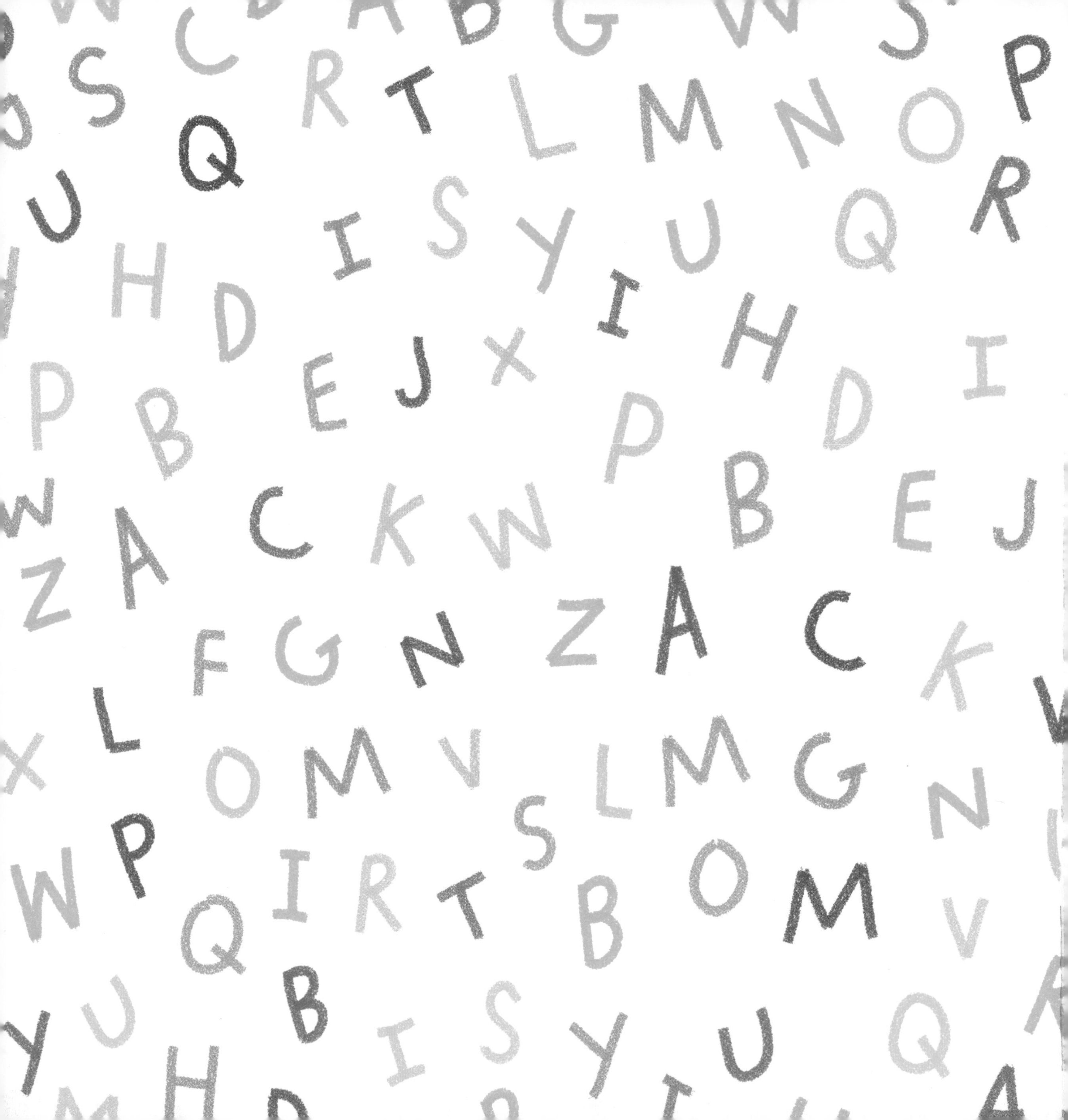

SCHOOL IS COOL!

STORY BY
SABRINA MOYLE

PICTURES BY
EUNICE MOYLE

ABRAMS APPLESEED • NEW YORK

Tomorrow's the first day of school!

What will it be like? How to begin?
It's your big day! Will you fit in?

You're worried kids
won't like your hair.

Or how you talk.
Or what you wear.

That SHAGGY 'do?

That **SPARKLING** voice?

Those **DAPPER** duds?

I like your choice!

But first things first:
Get out of bed.

Brush your bill,
and comb your head.

Hop on a bike
or in a car.

Feel free to catch
a shooting star!

SCHOOL BUS

We're here. You made it. Way to go!
Now find your teacher, say hello!

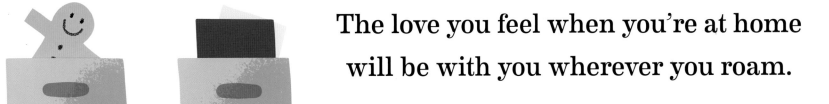

It can be sad to say goodbye.
But just you wait—the time will fly!

The love you feel when you're at home
will be with you wherever you roam.

Here's your cubby, desk, and seat.
This classroom's ours—let's keep it neat.

Circle time! Have something to share?
Raise your hand up in the air!

Paper, scissors, paint, and glue.
Let's share, take turns, try something new!

Make a project. Read a book.
Curl up in a cozy nook.

Recess time—let's go outside.

Run and swing! Zip down that slide!

Time for lunch. Where will you sit?
That face looks friendly—go for it.

DO YOU LIKE DUMPLINGS? SO DO I!
I LIKE NAAN AND SHEPHERD'S PIE!
LET'S TACO ABOUT IT!

What if your teacher
calls on you—
and the answer is five,
but you said . . .

2?

TODAY IS
MONDAY
THE MONTH IS
SEPTEMBER
THE DAY IS
5

Aa Bb C

See, school is where
your brain expands.

It stretches like a
rubber band!

Reading, math, and exercise—
they make you strong and super wise.

Together you'll make cool creations
by using your imaginations!

Best of all, school means new friends
who love to play, share, and pretend.

What you learn in school will last all year!
So how about a *hooray-for-school* cheer?

For teachers everywhere. You are the coolest!

The illustrations in this book were created digitally.

Library of Congress Control Number 2020939754
ISBN 978-1-4197-5110-3

Copyright © 2021 Hello!Lucky
Book design by Hana Anouk Nakamura

Printed and bound in China
10 9 8 7 6 5 4 3 2

For bulk discount inquiries, contact specialsales@abramsbooks.com.

ABRAMS The Art of Books
195 Broadway, New York, NY 10007
abramsbooks.com